Ready, Set, Cheer!

CHEERLEADING TRYOUTS AND COMPETITIONS

LISA MULLARKEY

Enslow Publishers, Inc.
40 Industrial Road
Box 398
Berkeley Heights, NJ 07922
USA

http://www.enslow.com

Many thanks to Emily Beggiato, Erika Lipinski, Alyssa Materazzo, Abby Michta, Sarah Mullarkey, and Bryanna Papcun for their contributions to this book.

Special thanks to Steven DeCasperis for many of the photos used here.

Copyright © 2011 by Enslow Publishers, Inc.

All rights reserved.

No part of this book may be reproduced by any means without the written permission of the publisher.

Library of Congress Cataloging-in-Publication Data

Mullarkey, Lisa.
 Cheerleading tryouts and competitions / Lisa Mullarkey.
     p. cm.—(Ready, set, cheer!)
 Includes bibliographical references and index.
 Summary: "Read about how to find the perfect squad for you to cheer on, handling tryouts, participating in competitions, and winning"—Provided by publisher.
 ISBN 978-0-7660-3539-3
 1. Cheerleading—Juvenile literature. I. Title.
 LB3635.M86 2010
 791.6'4—dc22
                                          2009044155

ISBN-13: 978-1-59845-201-3 (paperback)

Printed in the United States of America
052010 Lake Book Manufacturing, Inc., Melrose Park, IL

10 9 8 7 6 5 4 3 2 1

To Our Readers: We have done our best to make sure all Internet addresses in this book were active and appropriate when we went to press. However, the author and the publisher have no control over and assume no liability for the material available on those Internet sites or on other Web sites they may link to. Any comments or suggestions can be sent by e-mail to comments@enslow.com or to the address on the back cover.

 Enslow Publishers, Inc., is committed to printing our books on recycled paper. The paper in every book contains 10% to 30% post-consumer waste (PCW). The cover board on the outside of each book contains 100% PCW. Our goal is to do our part to help young people and the environment too!

Illustration Credits: Associated Press, pp. 4, 9, 12, 14, 21, 28, 32, 36, 40, 41, 44, 45; courtesy of Steven DeCasperis, pp. 1, 7, 24, 29, 44, 47; Nicole diMella/Enslow Publishers, Inc., pp. 19, 20, 34, 37, 42, 43, 45; Shutterstock.com, pp. 6, 10, 16, 23, 26; courtesy of Universal Cheerleaders Association, p. 31.

Cover Illustration: Courtesy of Steven DeCasperis.

CONTENTS

1. Finding Your Dream Squad . . . 5

2. Tackling Tryouts 13

3. Conquering Competitions . . . 25

4. Camp Champs 35

Words to Know 44

Learn More: Books and
    Web Sites 46

Index 48

1
FINDING YOUR DREAM SQUAD

Have you decided to become a cheerleader? Congratulations! Now comes the hard part. You must decide which squad is best for you. Will it be a recreational team? Maybe a competitive team? What's the difference? Read on!

Recreational: Everyone makes the squad. You do not have to try out. No one judges you. It is stress-free! This is a great choice if your focus is FUN! Are you new to the sport? A recreational (rec) team may be best for you.

TIP: Do you have a rec squad at your school or in your town? If not, you can ask your principal or the mayor about starting one.

Competitive: Many squads require you to try out. The competition is tough. You must excel in cheer, gymnastics, and dance skills. It can be stressful. Not everyone who tries

1 ★ FINDING YOUR DREAM SQUAD

For someone just starting out, a rec team is a good place to learn about cheering and have fun.

out will make the team. There are several different types of competitive (comp) teams:

★ **School:** You cheer for sports teams throughout the year. You boost morale and spread spirit. You help organize pep rallies.

★ **Youth League or Town Organization:** Your town probably has organized sports like Pop Warner Football. If you want to cheer for them, you must try out. Your squad will not cheer for school teams.

★ *All-Star Squads:* All-Stars do not cheer for teams. They compete against other All-Star squads. These cheerleaders are excellent tumblers, dancers, and stunters (cheerleaders who take part in throws or lifts). It is hard to become an All-Star. You have long practices several days a week. You travel a lot. Sometimes you will travel to different states to compete. Many All-Stars hope to cheer at the college and professional level.

Having trouble deciding which squad is best for you? Ask yourself why you want to cheer. Is it just for fun? Do you want to compete? Do you have a strong desire to win? Are you hoping to cheer in college? You may be an outstanding athlete and cheerleader. You may be the one that everyone watches. But that does not necessarily mean that a competitive team is the best choice for you.

Ten year-old Rachel Donnary agrees:

> I cheered on rec for a few years. Everyone made the squad. Then I decided to try out for the comp squad. When I made it, I felt proud. But after thinking about it,

No matter what kind of squad you are on, cheerleading gives you a chance to make friends who love to cheer too.

1 ★ FINDING YOUR DREAM SQUAD

I realized that I wouldn't have time to play with friends. I wouldn't be able to stay up late on the weekends because of early practices. I missed cheering with my friends on rec. I worried that I would feel pressured on the comp squad. I didn't want cheerleading to become something that I had to do. I didn't want to feel stressed out if I messed up. I decided to return to my old team and was glad I did.

Look Before Leaping (or Jumping!)

Before deciding if comp or All-Stars is best for you, think about the following:

★ *Funding:* All-Star squads are expensive. Many All-Stars take gymnastic and tumbling classes. They attend camps. All-Stars travel to competitions around the country. Airfare and hotels are expensive. Talk to your family about the expense.

★ *Health:* All-Stars and competitive cheerleaders are in great physical shape. They need to be. The routines are tough. Do you have the strength and stamina needed?

★ *Time commitment:* A competitive squad has many more practices than a rec squad does. You need time to devote to practices. Many are during the week. This interferes with homework. Are you an excellent student? Can you handle practices *and* homework?

★ *Dedication:* You will probably have to miss fun times with family and friends because of practices and competitions. Are you willing to do this?

These middle school cheerleaders are working with their coach. All kinds of cheerleading involve dedication and a time commitment.

★ *Attitude:* Do you have a winning attitude? Can you handle disappointment? Cheerleaders perform to win. Not everyone can win every time. Can you keep a positive attitude if you lose? Can you take constructive criticism from your coaches?

★ *Skills:* Do you have the time to prepare for tryouts?

★ *Showmanship:* Do you love the thrill of performing in front of large crowds? Do you love the spotlight?

Did you answer "yes" to all of these questions? Then you are ready to find your dream squad. Get ready to tackle tryouts and conquer competitions!

1 ★ FINDING YOUR DREAM SQUAD

Cheerleaders enjoy the thrill of performing in front of crowds.

TIP: Attend a performance of a squad you are interested in joining. Observe their skills and abilities. Do you think you have what it takes?

TIP: Keep in mind that most squads have tryouts once a year. If you are unsure about which way to go, consider joining a rec squad and trying out for a competitive squad later, when you feel more ready.

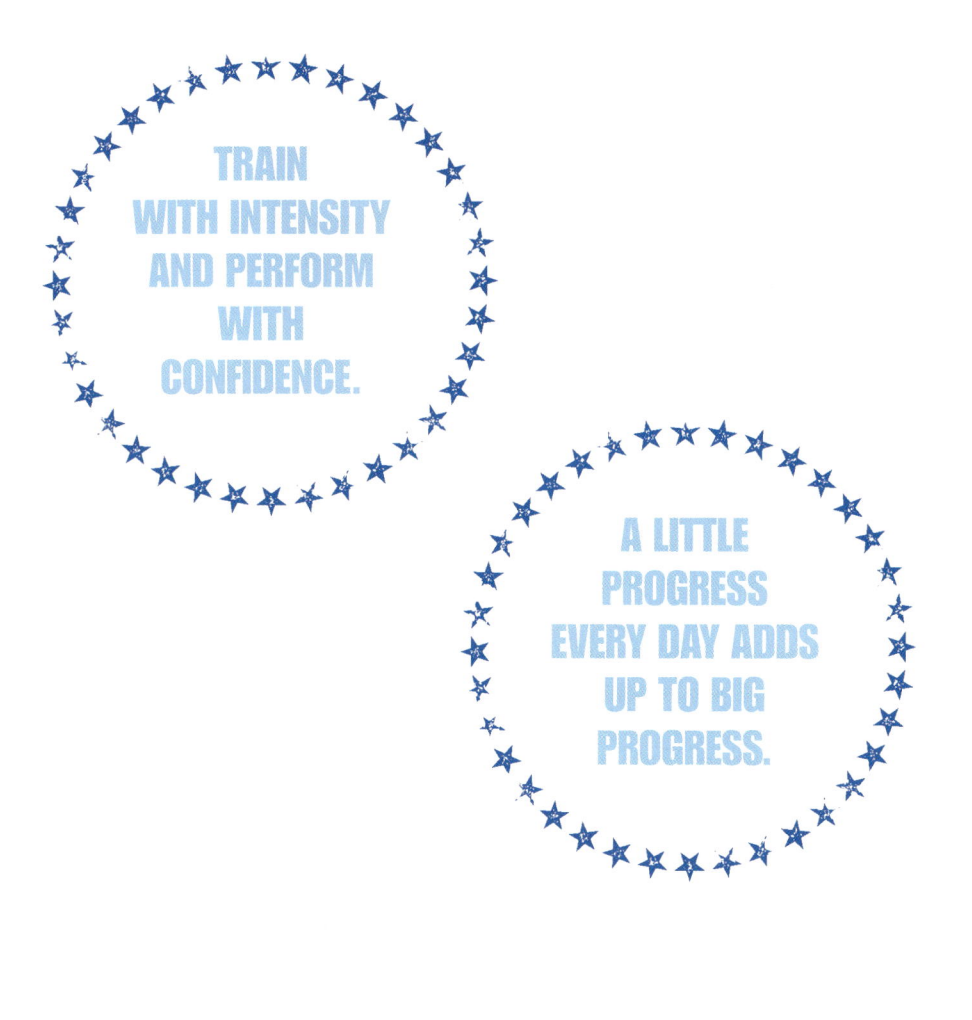

TRAIN WITH INTENSITY AND PERFORM WITH CONFIDENCE.

A LITTLE PROGRESS EVERY DAY ADDS UP TO BIG PROGRESS.

Practice makes perfect: Univerjseity of Nebraska cheerleaders work on their routine.

2
TACKLING TRYOUTS

Cheerleading skills are difficult. It takes time and practice to learn them. Planning months ahead for tryouts is a smart idea. The better prepared you are, the greater your chances are of making the team.

No one expects you to show up the day of tryouts and perform perfectly. Before the big day, you will be required to attend a clinic. It usually takes place in the spring. Clinics last a week. Everyone will learn and perform the same routine. It will be a new routine created just for tryouts. Because no one has seen the routine before, no one has an advantage.

Clinics are hard work. They are exhausting. Some girls decide it is too much work. They feel overwhelmed and quit. Do not be a quitter. Be prepared. How? Follow these tips.

2 ★ TACKLING TRYOUTS

"Cheerific" Clinic Tips

★ *Attend* every practice. If you skip one, it sends the message that you are not dedicated. Your coach may not allow you to try out if you miss a practice.

★ *Talk* to returning cheerleaders. They have been through tryouts already. Ask questions. Listen to their advice.

To be prepared for tryouts, it helps to practice dance and other skills. Clinics can help you get ready.

★ *Practice* at home in front of a mirror. Practice with friends. Practice, practice, practice!

★ *After each clinic*, go home and review what you have learned. Write down the words to each cheer and make notes of the motions.

★ *If coaches offer a mock tryout, do it.* At the end of your performance, you will not get a score. Instead, you will be told your strengths and weaknesses. Work on those.

★ *Get a copy of the routine's music.* Play the music over and over again. Close your eyes and picture the routine in your head.

★ *Be energetic.* Let your spirit soar. Coaches look for enthusiastic girls with A+ attitudes. Do not complain. Coaches want team players 24/7. Be one! Although coaches will not score your performance during the clinic, they will judge your attitude. The most technically accomplished cheerleaders are not always the ones picked.

Twelve-year coaching veteran Carol Whitmore agrees:

The number one thing I look for during tryouts? A girl with a positive attitude. One who has a willingness to learn. Anybody can be taught to be a cheerleader. I can work with them. Teach them. But I can't teach them to have a positive attitude. I can't make them want to learn. If the most skilled cheerleader has a poor attitude, I don't want her on my squad.

2 ★ TACKLING TRYOUTS

The Big Day

Tryouts can be scary. What if you make a mistake? Forget everything you were taught? Take a deep breath. Remind yourself how prepared you are. You worked hard during the clinic. You are ready to earn your spot on the squad. The best tip Whitmore can offer for tryouts? "Take a deep breath and smile, sparkle, shine."

The judges will score several skills that you learned in the clinic. What do judges look for? On p. 18 is a sample scorecard. It shows some things you will be judged on.

- ★ *Jumps:* There are many jumps in cheerleading. Concentrate on three for now: toe touch, pike jump, and front hurdler. Height is important. Soar!

A positive attitude is one of the main things coaches look for in choosing cheerleaders for the squad.

THE WINNING EDGE: TIPS FOR TRYOUTS

★ Wear comfortable clothes. Try to wear your team or school colors. Sneakers are a must.

★ Warm up and stretch.

★ Your hair should be up and away from your face.

★ Bring a bottle of water. Eat a light, healthy meal before you go.

★ Never let your smile fade. If you mess up during your performance, keep smiling. If you are disappointed with your performance, do not show it. Chances are you did better than you thought.

★ Skip the make-up. It can be distracting. If you feel you must wear something, think lip gloss.

★ Pay attention. Be respectful while others perform. Although coaches judge your individual performance, they look for team players.

★ Make eye contact with the judges during the whole performance.

★ Be polite and say thank you.

2 ★ TACKLING TRYOUTS

Number:

Note: Please make a comment in each category. For the Jump category, please specifically indicate which skill was performed. Your written comments will give us an indication of progress and a starting point for our choreographers.

Fundamentals	Maximum Points	Score	Comments
Cheer Motions (Sharpness, Arm Placement, Precision)	15		
Projection of Voice (Knowledge of Cheer, Clarity, Volume, Pitch)	5		
Jumps (Execution, Height, Landing, Overall Technique) **(Please indicate which jump was performed.)**	10		
Dance Technique (Rhythm, Arm Placement, Sharp Movements, Overall Effect)	10		
Showmanship (Spirit, Facial Expression, Energy)	5		
Appearance (Appropriate, Neat, Hair secure)	5		

This scorecard shows what skills the judges are looking for.

★ *Tumbling:* Not all squads require tumbling skills. However, tumbling is a bonus and will earn you higher marks. The most popular tumbles are cartwheels, round-offs, back handsprings and tucks. Try to master at least one. It adds an exciting part to your performance.

A back handspring is one of the most popular tumbling skills.

★ **Motions:** Make your chants tight. Quick, sharp motions are ideal. You will probably be taught chants to perform at tryouts. You will be judged on how sharp and tight your motions are. Remember: Short and snappy makes coaches happy!

2 ★ TACKLING TRYOUTS

Motions need to be strong and snappy.

★ **Voice projection:** Cheerleaders need to be loud. Do not scream or screech. When you shout your cheer, yell from your diaphragm and make your voice deep and clear. This sounds easy, but it takes some practice to get it right. When you are jumping around in a cheer and yelling at the same time, it is easy to become out of breath.

★ **Dance:** Work to remember the steps. Try to keep the rhythm and correct timing.

★ **Spiriting:** When you see cheerleaders jump and shout "Let's go," "We're Number 1," and "Go, team, go" while doing motions, it is called spiriting. Spiriting is perfect for transition times. You might be asked to do some spiriting when you try out. Have a short "spiriting routine" ready to perform.

★ **Facials:** Let your face tell a story. Your facial expressions, or "facials," get the crowd fired up. They impress the judges. No one wants to see a grumpy-looking cheerleader. Start by smiling. It is harder than it sounds. You must keep a smile on your face while performing difficult stunts. Wink. Give a head nod to show off your ribbons and ponytail. Open your mouth wide and raise your eyebrows to express yourself. Always match your facial expressions to your motions and chants.

TIP: If asked to do something you cannot, say that you are still learning that skill. You have not mastered it yet.

Cheerleader tryouts at the University of Nebraska. Cheerleaders have to smile even during difficult routines.

21

2 ★ TACKLING TRYOUTS

SUCCESS IS GETTING UP ONE MORE TIME THAN YOU FALL DOWN.

If you can do it with a spotter, tell them. It will help you get a higher score than you would if you skipped the skill.

And the Pom-Pom Goes To . . .

Thumbs up: The moment has arrived. The new squad members are announced. Your name is called! CONGRATULATIONS! Your hard work paid off. While it is normal to be excited, do not brag. Try to think about how the girls who did not make the squad might feel. Say something positive to people who congratulate you. Thank the judges.

Thumbs down: What if your name is not called? You will not be alone. Not everyone can make the squad. Did you try your hardest? If so, give yourself credit. You *do* have what it takes to be a cheerleader. This team was just not the best fit. Take a few minutes to collect your thoughts. Splash water on your face. If you need to cry, it is okay. But do not be a drama queen. Do not bad-mouth cheerleaders or judges. As hard as it may be, smile. Congratulate the new squad members. When you go home, treat yourself to a bubble bath. Have a sleepover party.

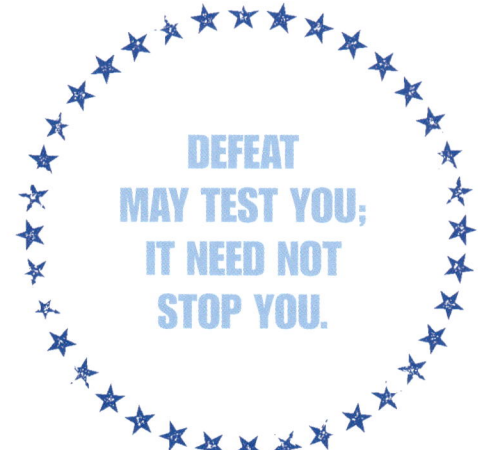

DEFEAT MAY TEST YOU; IT NEED NOT STOP YOU.

If you don't make the squad, it's natural to be disappointed. But it doesn't mean you won't succeed next time.

The next day, search for a new squad. The second time may be the charm.

If you don't make it but still want to be on that squad, don't be afraid to try out at the next opportunity. Often, the girl who comes back the next time to try again shows the coach that she is dedicated and determined—two qualities that make a great cheerleader.

3
CONQUERING COMPETITIONS

Competitions are a big part of cheerleading. It is a time for your squad to shine. It is time to prove that you have the right stuff. You will be amazed how many hours of practice you need to perfect a three-minute routine.

So Many Competitions, So Little Time

Before competing, your squad might attend a local competition just to watch. Some coaches have pizza parties so their squads can watch videos of different teams performing. After watching the routines, your squad might discuss the strengths and weaknesses of each routine.

If your squad is just starting to compete, you will begin by competing on the local level. This means that you

3 ★ CONQUERING COMPETITIONS

HERE ARE SOME FUN WAYS TO RAISE MONEY:

- ★ Organize a "fun run" and charge people to enter
- ★ Sell spirit items at games
- ★ Hold a "pet wash" (like a car wash, but for dogs!)
- ★ Collect change
- ★ Sell candy bars
- ★ Hold a "pajama day" at your school; kids have to pay for the right to wear pajamas to class
- ★ Hold a yard sale

Entering competitions can be expensive. Think about ways for your squad to earn money, such as a car wash—or even a pet wash!

will go to a competition in your state. It will not be too far from your home or school. As you improve, you move on to regional competitions (your part of the country) and then nationals. The national competitions are thrilling. You will go up against squads from all over the United States.

Many competitions have different divisions you can enter based on your squad's skill level. These divisions are *novice*, *intermediate*, *advanced*, and *elite*. If you are a new squad, you will probably start in the novice division. If your squad stays together for a long time and practices a lot, you could end up in the elite division one day.

Competitions are very expensive. You will need to raise money. Your coaches will decide which competitions are worthwhile and how much fundraising is needed. Since you will do a lot of fundraising, be creative! Go beyond bake sales and car washes.

Spice It Up!

Your routine will be *choreographed*. That means that each step, turn, and movement has to be created and thought out, one move at a time. Sometimes coaches choreograph the routines. Sometimes squads do it themselves. Many All-Star teams hire professional choreographers.

The routine will include many components. These include music, cheer, dance, tumbling, stunting, formations, and jumps. A choreographer must combine all of these components into a high-energy, electrifying routine. But you have the hard part. You must make it look easy.

3 ★ CONQUERING COMPETITIONS

Cheerleaders in Indiana practice before a competition. Choreographers plan the moves, and squads practice to perfect them.

28

Competition Day:
Tick Tock—Don't Watch the Clock!

Be prepared to do a lot of waiting around at the competition. If you are lucky, you will perform early in the day. If not, you may be in for a long wait. Be patient. Your time will come.

While waiting, you should warm up and stretch. After stretching, your squad might want to watch the other teams perform. Some teams decide not to watch. It makes them nervous. Your squad should decide before you go if you will (or won't) watch the other routines. If you do watch, be polite. Clap for them. Do not be critical of their performance. Show good sportsmanship at all times.

Before competing, it's important to stretch and warm up.

29

3 ★ CONQUERING COMPETITIONS

Nerves of Steel?

All cheerleaders get nervous before a competition. It is tough to know that all eyes will be on you. The trick is to not let your nerves show during your three-minute routine. To calm yourself down, try some deep-breathing exercises. Find a quiet place to sit. Inhale slowly through your nose. Breathe air deep into your lungs. Hold your breath for five seconds. Repeat several times. You will feel more relaxed.

TIP: Settle in for a long day with lots of water to keep hydrated. Pack snacks that will provide an energy boost. Think nuts, fresh fruit/veggies, and a bagel with cream cheese.

Judges watch a squad compete. It can be tough to perform when all eyes are on you.

UNIVERSAL CHEERLEADERS ASSOCIATION
JUDGING SHEET

EVENT NAME: _____ JUDGE NO. _____ TEAM NO. _____

TEAM NAME: _____ DIVISION _____

CHEER SECTION – 35 POINTS POSSIBLE

CROWD LEADING 15 POINTS _____
  Crowd Effective Material (Easy to Follow, Encourages Crowd Participation) (10)
  Use of Motions to Lead the Crowd (5)

INCORPORATIONS 15 POINTS _____
  Proper use of Skills to Effectively Lead the Crowd (5)
  Use of Signs or Poms or Megaphones (5)
  Execution of Incorporations (5)

OVERALL CHEER IMPRESSION 5 POINTS _____

MUSIC SECTION – 55 POINTS POSSIBLE

PARTNER STUNTS
  EXECUTION - Proper Technique, Form, Synchronization, Spacing   10 POINTS _____
  DIFFICULTY - Level of Skill, Number of Bases, Transitions, Variety   10 POINTS _____
    (Coed Divisions – unassisted vs. assisted coed stunts)

PYRAMIDS
  EXECUTION - Proper Technique, Form, Synchronization, Spacing   10 POINTS _____
  DIFFICULTY - Level of Skill, Number of Bases, Transitions, Variety   5 POINTS _____

TUMBLING
  EXECUTION - Proper Technique, Form, Synchronization, Spacing   5 POINTS _____
  DIFFICULTY – Synchronized Squad Tumbling, Level of Skill, Transitions   5 POINTS _____

JUMPS 5 POINTS _____
  Synchronized Squad Jumps, Jump Technique, Type of Jump, Synchronization, Spacing

DANCE 5 POINTS _____
  Sharpness, Motion Placement, Synchronization, Spacing

OVERALL PRESENTATION – 10 POINTS POSSIBLE

OVERALL EFFECT 10 POINTS _____
  Choreography, Transitions, Flow of Routine, Visual Appeal
  Age-Appropriate Material, Music Selection, Natural Appearance

100 POINTS POSSIBLE TOTAL _____

A sample evaluation form

3 ★ CONQUERING COMPETITIONS

Members of a winning squad celebrate at the national cheerleading championships.

32

Ready, Set, Compete!
Your squad is minutes away from its performance. Do a quick inspection of uniforms, hair, and makeup. Take a few minutes to visualize and go through the routine in your head. The big moment is finally here. Have fun!

Once you have wowed the judges and all squads have performed, you must wait again. The judges need time to tally your score.

Drum Roll, Please!
When the judges are about to announce the winners, the entire room becomes silent. Girls cross their fingers. Coaches take deep breaths. If you hear your squad's name announced, congratulations! Your hard work and effort paid off. If you did not get an award, you can be sure of one thing: the next competition is right around the corner.

RISKY BUSINESS?
Recent studies have shown that cheerleading can be a dangerous sport. New rules and better training for coaches are aimed at making cheerleading less risky. You need to play a part in preventing injuries by listening carefully to your coaches and following their instructions to the letter. Cheerleaders also need to pay attention to each other and look out for risky situations. Following the rules isn't just a good idea—it can keep you safe.

Camp is a great place to work on new skills with your squad.

4 CAMP CHAMPS

Many squads hold tryouts in the spring, just before summer vacation. If you make the squad, does it mean can you relax for the summer? Not necessarily—get ready for camp! This is a time to improve skills, learn the latest trends, and raise team spirit by bonding with your squad.

Cheer camp is not designed to get you in shape. You must be in tip-top shape before going. You do not want an injury to keep you from missing camp. It is important to exercise, stretch, and eat healthy in the off-season, too.

Which Camp Is Best?

There are different kinds of camps. Sleepaway camps are popular for squads. You live with your squad 24/7. Classes focus on improving your squad's skills. These camps are expensive. You pay for your room and food, too. Squads that compete a lot often choose this type of camp.

4 ★ CAMP CHAMPS

Girls at a cheerleading day camp

There are also day camps. Day camps are less expensive than sleepaway camps. You do not pay for rooms or food. Some day camps are open to individual cheerleaders. This way, if the rest of your squad cannot go, you still can. Research which type of camp is best for you.

Give me a P!

P is for Preparation! Be prepared for camp. One thing you *must* bring: a positive attitude.

You are there to learn and improve your cheers, jumps, tumbling, dancing, and motions. Be open to suggestions from the coaches. Ask questions. Take notes. Thank the coaches for their help. Show off your winning attitude and spirit!

What Should You Bring to Sleepaway Camp?

Use this checklist. Items marked with a * would be perfect for day camp, too:

- ★ Comfortable clothes: not too baggy, not too tight (shorts, tanks, sports bras)*
- ★ Appropriate cheer sneakers*
- ★ Extra shoes: flip-flops, sandals, etc. for other camp activities
- ★ Extra socks
- ★ Band-aids and ointment for blisters*
- ★ PJs
- ★ Pillow (check to see if linens are included)
- ★ Personal items: shampoo, toothpaste, deodorant
- ★ Sunscreen and bug spray (if outdoors)*
- ★ Small bag to carry stuff throughout day*
- ★ Disposable camera*
- ★ Small amount of money (for snacks, T-shirt)*
- ★ Healthy snacks*

A book and your favorite stuffed animal are good items to pack for sleepaway camp.

4 ★ CAMP CHAMPS

- ★ Refillable water bottle (write your name on it)*
- ★ Notebook and pen*
- ★ Favorite stuffed animal or good-luck charm
- ★ Sunglasses*
- ★ Flashlight
- ★ Sweatshirt for night
- ★ Swimsuit (if pool is available)*
- ★ Hair ties and gel to keep hair out of face*
- ★ Lip gloss (all that cheering makes your lips dry)*

What NOT to Bring

Leave valuables at home. Who wants to lose a laptop, cell phone, or digital camera? It happens. Since you cannot wear jewelry while cheering, do not pack any. If you wonder if certain items are allowed, ask.

MAKING MEMORIES

Attending camp is fun! Take lots of pictures with your disposable camera. Make a scrapbook. Have friends—new and old—autograph a piece of paper. Include it in your book.

Start Your Own Camp

Are you looking for a way to spread your spirit? Organize your own camp! The first thing you must decide is who your target audience will be. Do you want to have a camp for cheerleaders your own age? If so, invite cheerleaders from surrounding schools and All-Star squads. Do you want to have a camp for younger cheerleaders? This type of camp is a good one to start with. You can teach them skills you learned long ago. There are many possibilities. No matter what kind of camp you organize, you will need adult supervision. A qualified coach must be at camp at all times. You might also contact local colleges or a chapter of the Universal Cheerleaders Association or National Cheerleaders Association to see if they can find trained cheerleaders who can staff your camp for a reasonable fee.

PEN PALS

You will probably meet cheerleaders from different states—maybe even other countries! Jot down names and e-mail addresses of new friends in your notebook so you can keep in touch.

Get a Game Plan: Brainstorm

If your coach agrees, it is time to decide where the camp will be held: a school gym? a park? Decide what (if anything) you will charge the cheerleaders to attend. Will you provide food and water? Do you want crafts? Will you have music picked out and encourage cheerleaders to make up new routines? There is a lot to discuss. Give yourself plenty of time to plan. Get everyone on your squad involved. It is a team effort. Here are some things you should think about for the first day of camp: Who will . . .

- ★ Lead cheers and chants?
- ★ Type and copy the words?
- ★ Register campers?

4 ★ CAMP CHAMPS

These young girls are learning to cheer. Think about holding a day camp as a fundraiser for your squad.

★ Make signs and posters?

★ Be in charge of crafts?

★ Lead warm-ups?

★ Be responsible for music?

★ Give out the awards (and decide who gets which one)?

★ Organize getting-to-know-you games?

★ Share the history of the spirit stick (a decorated stick given to the camper or group with the most spirit)?

TIP: If this is your first year running a camp, start small. Consider a one-day camp with a theme such as "Reach for the Stars."

Sample Schedule

★ 9:00–9:30 Check in (Let girls work on a craft at a Spirit Table)

★ 9:30–9:45 Stretch and warm up

★ 9:45–10:00 Getting-to-know-you game

- ★ 10:00–10:30 Cheers and chants
- ★ 10:30–11:30 Skills (focus on jumps, tumbles, beginner stunts)
- ★ 11:30–11:45 Game/activity
- ★ 11:45–12:30 Lunch
- ★ 12:30–1:30 Dance routines (Share your dance routine. Break girls into smaller groups. Have each group make up a new routine to predetermined music.)

High school cheerleaders catch a participant in their camp program. This squad bought new uniforms with the money they earned from the camp.

4 ★ CAMP CHAMPS

★ 1:30–2:00 Spirit activity/craft

★ 2:00–3:00 Share dance routines; give out awards

You now know everything you need to know to tackle tryouts and conquer competitions. As they say in cheerleading: Bring it on!

The spirit stick is an important cheerleading tradition. Make sure to tell your campers about it!

FLIP OVER THESE FLOPS!

Often a team will wear the same t-shirts or hair ribbons to show unity and spirit. Have your squad make these flip-flops to show yours.

WHAT YOU NEED:
Pair of flip-flops, ribbon or fabric in team colors, scissors

WHAT YOU DO:
1. Cut strips of fabric or ribbon into four-inch lengths with various widths.
2. Tie the fabric onto the top (starting in middle and working out) of the flip-flop by making a knot. Repeat until the strap is full.

TIP: Make a pair for your coach!

WORDS TO KNOW

choreography (core-ee-OG-ra-fee)—The creation and arrangement of the movements in a dance or routine. Routines are choreographed (CORE-ee-o-graft).

diaphragm (DIE-a-fram)—The thin layer of muscles that separates the chest from the abdomen. It helps control breathing.

elite (a-LEET)—The highest level of cheerleading competition.

excel—To be very good at something.

mock tryout—A tryout that is not the real thing but gives you a chance to experience the situation.

novice *(NAH-vis)*—The beginning level of cheerleading competition.

stamina *(STAM-ih-nuh)*—Endurance; the ability to be active for a long time without getting tired.

stunt—An activity that involves lifting or throwing a cheerleader.

LEARN MORE

BOOKS

Carrier, Justin, and Donna McKay. *Complete Cheerleading*. Champaign, Ill.: Human Kinetics, 2006.

Gruber, Beth. *Cheerleading for Fun*. Minneapolis: Compass Point Books, 2004.

Jones, Jen. *Cheer Competitions: Impressing the Judges*. Mankato, Minn.: Capstone Press, 2008.

Maurer, Tracy Nelson. *Competitive Cheerleading*. Vero Beach, Fla.: Rourke Publishing, 2006.

WEB SITES

Activity TV: Cheerleading
<http://www.activitytv.com/cheerleading-for-kids>

American Youth Football and Cheer
<http://www.americanyouthfootball.com/cheerleading.asp>

Varsity Official Site
<http://www.varsity.com>

INDEX

A
all-star squad, 6, 8–9, 27, 38
attitude, 9, 15, 36

C
camp, 8, 35–42
cheer, 27, 36
choreography, 27
clinic, 13–15, 16
competition, 8, 9, 25, 27, 29, 30, 33, 42
competitive (comp) team, 5–6, 7, 8, 11

D
dance, 5, 6, 20, 27, 36, 41, 42
day camp, 36, 37–38
Donnary, Rachel, 7–8

F
facials, 20–21
flip-flops, 43
formations, 27
fundraising, 26, 27

G
gymnastics, 5, 8

J
jumps, 16, 27, 36, 41

L
lift, 6

M
motions, 15, 19, 20, 21, 36
music, 27, 39, 40, 42

P
pep rally, 6
performance, 11, 15, 17, 18, 29, 33
Pop Warner Football, 6

R
recreational (rec) team, 5, 8, 11
routine, 8, 13, 15, 20, 25, 27, 29, 30 33, 39, 41–42

S
school team, 6
sleepaway camp, 35, 36, 37–38
spirit, 6, 15, 36, 43
spiriting, 20
sportsmanship, 29
spotter, 22
start a camp, 38–42
stretch, 17, 29, 35, 40
stunt, 6, 21, 27, 41

T
throws, 6
tryout results, 22–23
tryouts, 9, 11, 13–16, 18–22
tryout tips, 17
tumbler, 6
tumbling, 8, 18, 27, 36

V
voice projection, 20

W
Whitmore, Carol, 15, 16